Holy Family School
South Bend, **Date Due**

CT 16 '72			
NOV 6 '72			
MAR 28 74			
SEP 21 7			
JAN 28 '80			
MAR 18 '80			
NOV 25 '80			

DEMCO NO. 38-298

The Sioux Are Coming

also by

WALTER O'MEARA

The First Northwest Passage

The Sioux Are Coming

WALTER O'MEARA

Illustrated by Lorence Bjorklund

HOUGHTON MIFFLIN COMPANY BOSTON 1971

For Michael and Alexander

CONTENTS

flight

1

AT THEIR CAMP on the Otter River, Odena was making raspberry cakes for the winter. She dipped her wooden ladle into a kettle of boiling raspberries and spread patches of the rosy syrup on a sheet of birch bark. After they had dried in the sun, she would stack the cakes and tie them in neat bundles for storing.

Odena poured a few very small cakes from the last of the syrup in her ladle.

"These will be for Ona," she said to her daughter Nitana.

Nitana turned her doll, which was cleverly made from bits of bright cloth stuffed with moss, toward the tiny cakes and said: "Do you hear, Ona? These are for you. They will be very good with your rice and fish soup."

Wanito, her brother, looked up from the arrow shaft he was smoothing with a piece of sandstone.

"When are we going home?" he asked abruptly.

"Your father will decide," Odena answered, "when he returns from the trader's fort."

After the wild-rice harvest, their father, Kawa, had decided to camp on the Otter for a while and hunt meat for the winter. At first Wanito, who was twelve, and Nitana, who was two years younger, were happy in their hunting camp. But now they had become bored. They missed the bustle and excitement of the Indian village where they lived for most of the year.

"I hope it is soon," Wanito said, sighting down the arrow shaft to see if it was straight. "I am tired of playing with Nitana."

Nitana's answer to this was simple. "Boys," she said, "are dumb."

"Children!" Odena said, a little severely. "Why should you complain? What could be better than this?"

It was indeed a pleasant spot, this little clearing in which they had pitched their lodge. And especially now, in the month of Shining Leaves. The late sun was warm on the river bank and the sweet smells of fall filled the air. Pleasant, and peaceful, and safe.

As safe, that is, as one could hope to feel. For an Indian, no matter how brave, could never be quite free from fear. He could never be sure that some danger might not lurk around the next bend of the river. Or over the hill. Or beyond a turn in the trail. So everyone was startled and a little frightened when Wanito said suddenly: "Somebody is coming!"

They listened intently, at the same time glancing backward toward the forest where, if necessary, they might hide. What they heard was the faint sound of voices upriver. Finally a canoe slid into view from behind a clump of alders.

"It's Big Turtle," Wanito said, disappointed that it was not something more exciting.

Big Turtle was Kawa's brother, who also had been in a hunting camp on the Otter. He was not alone. He had with him his wife Dawn Sky, his little daughter Spilt-her-berries, and a new baby.

"Where is Kawa?" he called, without other greeting.

Odena did not answer at once. She was not fond of her brother-in-law and his rude ways. She continued to pour raspberry cakes until her ladle was empty. Then she walked down to the water's edge. But before she spoke to Big Turtle, she greeted Dawn Sky and Spilt-her-berries. Then she exclaimed over the baby, who was regarding her solemnly from his cradleboard: *"Saum!* How fast he grows!" Finally, taking notice of Big Turtle, she said, "My husband has gone to the trader's house, to have his gun repaired."

"When will he return?"

"Soon."

"It had better be very soon," Big Turtle said grimly. "The Sioux are coming."

Odena looked at Big Turtle silently for a while,

then said, "You should be ashamed of yourself, Big Turtle, frightening the children so."

"Yes," Nitana said to Ona. "Do not be afraid."

But Nitana clutched her doll a little tighter to her breast and drew closer to her mother.

"I am not afraid of the Sioux," Wanito declared. "Besides, I am not a child."

Wanito had already killed small game with his father's gun, and considered himself quite grown-up. In only a few years, he would go on war parties. It was not a man's part to fear the Sioux or, for that matter, anything else — except maybe the Windigo.

"There are always such tales in the month of Shining Leaves," he added, repeating something he had heard his father say.

And this was true. In September, when the Sioux were accustomed to take the war road, rumors of their coming always ran through the country of the Ojibway. And often enough the rumors proved true.

For a long, long time, the Ojibway and Sioux had been at war. Wanito had often heard his father tell of the ancient days when the Sioux owned all the hunting grounds now in the hands of the Ojibway. They were a brave people, but the Ojibway came from the rising sun and drove them westward, onto the treeless plains.

There the Sioux took to the horse and hunted buffalo for food, and for skins to cover their lodges. They grew strong and warlike again. Now they delighted in making raids on their old enemy, the Ojibway. Every fall they spread terror through the country beyond Kitchi Gumi, the great inland sea white men called Lake Superior: Ojibway country.

And now, Big Turtle said, these fierce plains Indians were once again coming from the west. Their canoes were everywhere on the lakes and rivers. A strong band was coming down the Otter itself, surprising Ojibway families in the rice beds, killing the men and carrying off the women and children. Big Turtle himself had talked with some of those who had escaped.

"Where are you going?" Odena asked him. "Where do you hope to find safety?"

"At the fort," Big Turtle said. "Even the Sioux will not brave the trader's guns and brass cannon."

The enemy, he said, was not far away. They were heavily loaded with booty and making slow progress. But there was nothing to stop them.

"They will be along soon enough," he added. "I have warned you."

With that, he swung out into the current and paddled away. Odena watched until his canoe was lost to sight behind some low-hanging willows.

"Pay no attention to Big Turtle," she said. "He has the heart of a rabbit. Come, Nitana, help me with the raspberry cakes."

She went back to her kettle, and later on prepared an evening meal of little maize cakes flavored with pounded hazelnuts. But she was oddly quiet, and Wanito saw her go several times to the river bank and look downstream in the direction from which his father would come.

Dusk gathered in the black spruce forest and began to fill the clearing in which their lodge stood. Then darkness fell suddenly and Wanito, for all his brave words, felt afraid — not for himself, but for his mother and sister . . . The ferocity of the Sioux spared no one.

He lay awake for a long time in the darkness of the lodge, listening to the low, unearthly moan of a great owl somewhere in the depths of the woods. Old men grew silent when they heard that sound. It was an evil omen, they said, and Wanito had often laughed to himself at their fears. But on this night he did not laugh.

2

The white morning mist was still rising from the water when Kawa's canoe appeared on the river. Odena thought: *He has been traveling all night. He has heard the bad news.*

But if this was indeed the case, Kawa gave no sign of it. Odena had cooked some deer meat and wild rice for him, and he ate this silently and quickly — as if he had been a long time without food. Then he said:

"It is time for us to return to our village."

Kawa said this quietly, but Wanito guessed the hidden fear in his father's words. They, too, were going to seek the safety of the trader's fort, under whose strong walls their village stood.

"Big Turtle came by yesterday," Wanito ventured to remark. "He said he was fleeing from the Sioux."

"I know," Kawa said. "I passed him on Caribou Lake."

He motioned Wanito to step a little apart from his mother and sister.

"I will tell you this, my son," he said in a low voice. "Big Turtle spoke with a straight tongue. The Sioux are everywhere on the war road. They have even attacked the Cree. On the White River they burned three of our villages and killed everyone. They did not spare the young."

"Big Turtle said their canoes are on this river — only a few days' journey away."

"He spoke the truth."

"I am not afraid of them," Wanito said. "I do not fear the Sioux."

"My son," Kawa said, "how long do you think you and I could stand against a whole war band?"

Kawa's question made Wanito feel taller — like a warrior. *You and I,* his father had said.

"Anyhow," Wanito said, "I am not afraid of them."

Kawa laughed. "Come!" he called. "We have no time to waste."

He gave each member of the family a task to perform, and they all set to work at once. As it was the women's duty, Odena and Nitana took down the lodge, so that the birch bark with which it was covered might be saved. They rolled the bark up neatly and carried it into the forest. There they hid it beneath the roots of a fallen spruce tree.

In the meantime, Kawa and Wanito went deep into the woods and built a well-concealed scaffold on which to store furs and provisions. Here they placed the meat Kawa had dried and a pack of beaver pelts he had trapped. The pelts were of very fine quality, the fur dark and silky. They would buy many yards of scarlet cloth, brass kettles, brightly colored beads, blankets, and ammunition for Kawa's gun at the trader's house.

The wild rice they had harvested they stored in a *cache,* a hole dug in the ground and lined with birch bark. When all was finished, Kawa said, "I wish that

we might at least take the beaver pelts with us, for they are very valuable. But we will have to travel light if we are to keep ahead of the Sioux."

They all worked so swiftly that the sun was scarcely an arrow's length above the trees when they were ready to leave. But first Kawa contrived a trick to fool the Sioux. On a piece of birch bark he traced a picture with a bit of charcoal. It showed an empty tipi, with no bones around the lodge fire. This meant that the people in the tipi were without food. Then he drew a picture of a canoe in which there were four figures — a large catfish, two small catfish, and an eagle. Kawa was of the catfish clan. So were Wanito and Nitana. But Odena was of the eagle totem. So Kawa's pictures were a message. It meant that he and his family had run out of food. They had left their camp to seek better hunting elsewhere. The Ojibway often left such messages behind for friends or relatives to read.

Kawa folded the message and placed it in a split stick. Then he thrust the stick into the ground, slanting it so that it pointed up the river — in the opposite direction from the one they would really take.

"The Sioux will read it," Kawa said, "and maybe they will be fooled."

Then he eased their canoe into the water. It was a lovely canoe, its lines clean and sweet, its bark still honey-colored, the pitch on its seams amber-hued, for it was quite new. Kawa had built it himself, and nobody in his band could equal his skill with the crooked knife of the canoe maker.

The loading was done quickly, for there was little to stow: blankets, cooking pot, Kawa's gun and medicine bag, an ax, a couple of woven cedar bags crammed with spare clothing and household articles, food for only a few days. And Waboos.

Waboos (whose name meant Rabbit) had not been very helpful during the preparations for leaving. Like any puppy, he had got under foot a good deal; and now that everyone was ready to go, he ran away and barked defiantly when Wanito tried to catch him.

"All right, stupid dog," Wanito said. "You can stay. The Sioux will put you in their kettle."

"No! No!" Nitana shrieked. "Here, Waboos —
come here!"

It was she who caught him at last. With Waboos
under one arm and Ona in the other, she climbed
into the middle of the canoe beside her mother.

Kawa picked up two paddles. The shorter one, the
bow paddle, he handed to Wanito.

He said nothing, but to Wanito this was a very important thing. Odena, who was a strong and skillful
paddler, had always worked the canoe with Kawa.
But now he, Wanito, was going to take his mother's
accustomed place in the bow. It was as if Kawa had
said, "Here, Wanito, this hard and dangerous journey will be work for men."

Kawa strewed a little tobacco on the water to win
the good will of the Water Spirits. As it floated
downstream, he sang a short prayer to the Kitchi-
Manitou for a safe arrival at the trader's fort.

Then he and Wanito dipped their blades into the
slow current of the river. As they slipped away from
their deserted camp, Wanito cast a quick glance behind him. The river was empty, except for a couple
of wood ducks circling near the shore.

"The Sioux will never catch us now," he said. "Even with stolen Ojibway canoes."

But Kawa was silent.

3

The clear brown water of Otter River flowed deep and quiet, and their canoe glided swiftly between its high banks of spruce and tamarack. It was very peaceful on that shadowy river road through the forest. One could almost forget that the Sioux, too, were traveling it — perhaps not very far behind.

Wanito's paddle dipped steadily in time with Kawa's and the canoe made a pleasant little leap forward — almost like a live thing — at the end of each stroke. Sometimes a flock of ducks clattered off the water ahead of them. Once a doe and her fawn watched them with burning eyes from the bank. Nitana sang a little lullaby to Waboos, who was growing restless.

Then, quite suddenly, the river broke out of the deep woods into rough country sparsely timbered.

The river became shallow, so that Wanito could see the sunlight rippling over the pebbles on the sandy bottom. It flowed faster, too, sometimes breaking into riffles of white water. Short stretches of rapids tossed and buffeted the canoe.

It was exciting to shoot the rapids, and a little dangerous at this time of year, even for an Indian. The water was low and swift, and it took all of Kawa's skill to avoid hitting some of the rocks that lay just below the surface. Then they heard ahead of them the sound of a long rapids that not even Kawa dared to run. It was time for them to make their first carry.

At the head of a well-worn portage trail, everyone got out. Kawa threw the canoe, bottom up, over his head and started off at a kind of trot. Wanito and Odena followed with the packs. Nitana trailed after them, with Waboos bringing up the rear.

At the far end of the portage they had their midday meal. They ate their cold maize cakes and smoked meat hastily, taking care that no telltale bits of food were left for the Sioux to see. And now, for the first time, Kawa talked about their situation.

"Before nightfall," he said, "we shall portage around the Falls of the Manitou and make camp. We will be safe there for the night. Even though the Sioux may be close behind us, they will not dare to cross the Manitou Portage in the dark, for it is a difficult and dangerous carry. And long before they can cross it in the morning, we shall be on our way."

The Sioux, he added, were perhaps no nearer than two or three days' journey away. They were poor canoemen, used only to horses and skin boats, and they traveled slowly . . . Still, it would be foolhardy to waste time.

"Tomorrow," he said, "we must reach Caribou Lake, and the next day the trader's fort."

"Do you hear that, Waboos?" Nitana asked. "You are going to have some friends to play with."

"Girls are silly," Wanito said. "Even my own sister."

Dusk was filling the clefts and hollows in the rocks along the shore when they heard ahead of them the roar of the Manitou Falls. It was a very high falls, plunging straight down, over a ledge of granite, for the height of six men. You could not talk above its thunder. Its spray wet the very tops of the trees.

Because it lay around a wide bend of the river, a canoeman came upon the Manitou Falls suddenly. If he were caught in the middle of the stream, his canoe might easily be seized by treacherous crosscurrents. Then, struggle as he might to reach shore, he would be drawn faster and faster toward the brink of the falls. This had once happened to some fur traders, and three crosses now stood beside the portage trail to mark the mishap. White men called the portage "Deadman's Carry."

But Kawa, who knew every rip and eddy in the Otter, had no trouble in bringing his canoe safely to the portage landing. This time, the trail was very steep and rough, and they had to carry their canoe and baggage over much of it in darkness. Everyone was exhausted when, at last, they reached the campsite below the falls.

They did not dare to build a fire, so they ate cold maize cakes and smoked meat again, with a few dried blueberries for dessert. Then Odena spread blankets under the overturned canoe for Nitana and herself.

Kawa said to Wanito, "I have been too long without sleep. You will have to keep the first watch. When the moon reaches the top of her journey across the sky, wake me up."

He handed Wanito his gun, rolled up in his blanket, and fell asleep at once. Wanito sat down on a flat boulder with his father's gun across his knees. Keeping guard over his family made him feel very important, but at the same time very sober.

The trees were black against the rising moon, and the night silent, except for the distant sound of the Manitou Falls. As Wanito listened to this sound, he could hear more and more clearly wild laughter and silvery voices calling back and forth in the darkness. This, as every Indian knew, was the laughter and chatter of the Water Spirits frolicking in the mist below the falls.

After a while the voices of the Water Spirits lulled Wanito to sleep. He awoke with a start. To keep from dozing off again, he began to walk up and down the edge of the river. When the moon was high overhead, he awoke Kawa.

4

The first still light of dawn was on the water when they launched their canoe again. By the time the sun was up, they were close enough to Caribou Lake to hear the loons greeting the new day with their mad cries.

"I think there may be a little wind today," Kawa said. "We will cross as much of this lake as we can before it rises."

Kawa knew how difficult, and even dangerous, it was to travel in a frail bark canoe across a large body of rough water. He also knew that the wind seldom blew hard before midday. So he was anxious to get started on the long journey down Caribou. He strewed a little tobacco on the water and asked Kitchi-Manitou, the Great Spirit, to give them a safe passage.

"You have made this lake," he prayed, "and you have made us, your children. Let the water remain calm, while we pass over it in safety."

And the Manitou, it seemed, did not fail to hear Kawa's prayer. The Otter River widened to a deep, slow channel where it emptied into Caribou Lake, winding through beds of tall reeds from which clouds of waterfowl rose as they slipped by. When, quite suddenly, the whole broad expanse of the lake opened before them, not a ripple disturbed its shining surface.

"We will be safe at the trader's fort tomorrow," Kawa said.

But Wanito did not fail to observe that, even while Kawa said this so confidently, he cast a quick glance at some wispy clouds on the western line of the sky. The Indians called them "wind clouds."

5

Caribou Lake stretched a hard day's journey northward before it emptied into the even larger Lake of Pines. It was strewn with tall, rocky islands among which a canoe might easily become lost, and its shores were often broken by deep bays.

Along its eastern shore lay the shortest route to Pine Portage, where the trader's fort stood. It was the canoe road that both the Indians and the white fur traders used. Kawa knew that the Sioux, too, would come this way; but there was no time to be lost, so he decided to risk taking it.

Morning is the time when everything wild is out flying, swimming, running, hunting, frolicking in the freshness of the new day. On all sides, trout leaped out of the clear water in search of breakfast. In a shallow bay filled with water lilies a cow moose and her calf raised their heads to look up for a moment, then clambered up the bank and crashed into the woods. Noisy flocks of ducks and coots

wheeled up against the pink sky. A kingfisher dived from an overhanging branch and came up dripping, with a small fish.

Nitana exclaimed with delight at all these splendid sights. She held Ona up to see them, too. But Wanito, like his father, paid them no heed. He looked straight ahead and pulled his paddle through the water with the quick, steady strokes of an Ojibway canoeman.

The Sioux, he was thinking, might even now be crossing the Manitou Portage.

Toward midday a little wind arose, but it was at their backs and caused them no trouble. It helped, in fact, to speed them through the wavelets stirred up on the broad surface of Caribou Lake. Then, quite suddenly, the wind veered, as it often did on these large inland lakes, and Kawa judged it best to head for quieter waters, near the lee shore. After some easy paddling there, they came to a deep, wide bay. And here they must leave the friendly protection of the shore and strike out across open water.

"But first we will eat," Kawa said. "This will not be a crossing to make on an empty stomach."

They brought their canoe alongside a flat, smooth rock. Odena and Nitana got out the cooking kettle and food bag. While Odena was making a fire, Kawa and Wanito paddled into the bay to fish. Kawa tossed out a hook baited with a bit of old red blanket, taking a twist of the basswood line around his wrist, so that the bait would dart through the water with each stroke of his paddle. They had scarcely gone ten canoe lengths before they hooked a fine fish, and shortly afterward three more.

Odena quickly cleaned the fish, while Wanito cut four green sticks and split them at one end. Into these sticks Odena placed the fish, then propped them before the fire, over which a kettle of wild rice was already boiling. Nitana turned the fish before the coals, so that all sides were nicely browned. When everything was ready, Odena served the wild rice in birch bark dishes and placed a *makuk* of maple sugar on the flat rock. She passed each of them a whole fish on the end of a pointed stick. They sprinkled sugar on both their fish and rice, and had a fine hot meal to prepare them for crossing the bay. They did not waste any time, however, for who could tell how close the Sioux might be? Besides, the wind was beginning to kick up little whitecaps on the open water. And the sky was clouding over.

6

By the time they were ready to cross the bay, the wind had shifted still more, so that it now blew directly from the shore. Kawa decided to head straight across the open water, taking the waves broadside.

"It looks dangerous," he explained to Wanito, "but it is the safest way."

At first, however, it seemed anything but safe. Nitana gave a little shriek and clutched Ona tighter each time the canoe rose to the crest of a wave, hung there for a moment, then slid into the trough. But so skillfully did Kawa manage that only a little water splashed into the canoe.

Yet, not even Kawa could foretell the sudden peril into which a broad, squall-swept lake could plunge the most expert canoeman. All at once, without warning, the wind veered again, this time so vio-

lently that it seemed to snatch the canoe in a giant fist
and spin it around, straight into the teeth of a huge
roller. The bow plunged into the water and Wanito
was drenched from hair to moccasins. The wave
poured over the sides, and Odena bailed frantically
with the cooking kettle. Nitana, too terrified even to
shriek, crouched over Waboos and Ona to protect
them from the deluge.

Another great wave lifted the canoe, and then another, driving it into an angry confusion of wide-open
water. Rain — cold, stinging rain — came with the
gale. They were in the grip, Wanito knew, of a
squall that no paddler was strong enough or skillful
enough to battle. They had only one chance to live
through it. They must run straight before the wind.

At such a time, Wanito had learned from Kawa,
there was but one thing for the bow paddler to do. He
must keep paddling straight ahead. Now only Kawa
could bring the canoe back on course as each roller
seized it and tried to swing it broadside to the wind.
If he failed just once, they would capsize and perish.
But Kawa did not fail. Over and over, at exactly the
right moment, he allowed the canoe to turn slightly

at the top of each wave, but only enough to prevent the water from pouring over the sides. Odena, indeed, had little to do with her bailing kettle. And Nitana recovered enough courage to comfort Waboos and Ona, and tell them not to be afraid.

But Wanito heard his father singing a prayer to the Kitchi-Manitou, and he knew that the danger had not yet passed. Their canoe had not turned over, or broken apart. They were still alive, at least. But at every paddle stroke they were being driven farther and farther from shore, out into the raging lake. And there was no possible way they could turn about and run for the shelter of land.

Then, through the blur of rain and spume, they did see land — land and disaster.

Directly ahead loomed one of the many islands that lay along the shore of Caribou Lake. It rose like a solid wall of rock — a wall against which the waves hurled themselves in a wild fury of foam and spray. Wanito knew well that their canoe was about to be dashed to pieces. Now even Kawa's skill and strength could not save them. He himself paddled straight ahead, as hard as he could, as Kawa had taught him to do — no matter what the weather, no matter what the danger. There was nothing else to do.

"Wanito — get ready to jump!"

The wind carried his father's shout through the storm. Wanito laid his paddle across the gunwales and tried to peer through the curtain of rain. Then he saw it. Kawa's keen eyes had found a chance, a small hope, a prayer of survival. It was a little strip of sandy beach at the foot of the towering wall of rock.

Wanito knew what his father's shout meant. Kawa was going to try and set the canoe down on the beach broadside. To drive straight into it would be almost as bad as plunging into the rocks. But if, at precisely the right moment, with a strong, sure twist of the paddle, he could take the wind broadside, they might be saved. Even the canoe might be saved.

He knew his own part well. Often, when approaching land, Kawa would turn the canoe until, lifted gently by a wave, it would drop sideways into the shallow water offshore. Then, almost at the last moment, Wanito would swing himself out on the windward side, without letting go, so as to steady the canoe and prevent it from landing too hard against the shore.

He had never done this in a storm before, but when Kawa called on him to leave the canoe, he would know just what to do. And how to do it. He waited.

"Now — jump!"

Kawa's shout came just as the canoe swung suddenly about and, after hanging for a moment at the top of a great roller, began to slide into the trough. At almost the same instant, Wanito went overboard. The wave swept over his head with such force that the canoe was wrenched from his grasp. Through the roar of the surf he heard a splintering, tearing sound. A second wave picked him up and hurled him against the shore. Something struck his head, and he heard nothing more.

on the island

1

*W*HEN *W*ANITO came to, he saw Odena and Nitana struggling to drag Kawa out of the surf. He shook his head to clear it. He scrambled to his feet and stumbled across the beach to help them. Together, they got Kawa onto higher ground, where the waves could not wash over him. Odena began to clear the sand and a little blood from his face. After a while, Kawa opened his eyes, looked around, and groaned.

"The canoe, Wanito," he said weakly. He tried to

get up, but his legs gave way under him. He fell on his back. "The canoe . . ."

Wanito ran to the water's edge. One look told him what had happened. The beach was not at all as smooth as it had appeared from the lake. Jagged boulders lay just below the water, and some projected above the sand. Their canoe had struck one of these boulders with such force that all of them, including Waboos, had been thrown clear of the water. The canoe was broken completely in two.

Every wave that crashed in was now battering the halves into still smaller pieces. But Wanito saw that some of the baggage was still wedged in the wreckage. He plunged into the water between rollers and dragged out what he could. While he threw things clear of the wreck, Nitana ran with them to a high spot on the beach. When Wanito tossed Ona to her, she paused to straighten her doll's small beaded dress and comfort her a little.

"Poor little thing!" she said. "Don't cry, Ona."

After everything in the wreck, including both paddles, had been got ashore, Wanito dived into the shallow water for things that had sunk. He found

Kawa's gun, the ax, and the brass cooking kettle.
Then he went back through the rain to tell his father
the bad news about the canoe.

2

They were too worn out that night even to talk
about their miserable plight. They crowded together
for warmth on a couple of moose skins, with a wet

blanket over them, and fell asleep in the rain.

When they awoke at daybreak, the rain had stopped and bright little waves washed lazily onto the beach where they had come to grief. It was the way of such squalls to go as quickly as they came, leaving behind them clear skies and gentle breezes. But, although the day promised to be a beautiful one, there was not much to be cheerful about. Only Odena could find a little hope in what had plainly become a very bad situation.

"At least, we are still alive," she said. "And we are all together."

Kawa, whose swollen knee was giving him a great deal of pain, grimaced but said nothing. All at once he, who had always been the family's provider and protector, was the helpless one. And because of this he was morose and cast down.

"Somebody will be along soon to take us off this wretched island," Odena added, trying to cheer everyone up.

"Yes," Nitana said, echoing her mother as usual. "Our relatives will come for us."

Kawa gazed at his little daughter, and Wanito

saw his face darken. He knew what his father was thinking.

"Somebody will be along, sure enough," he said to himself. "But it will probably be the Sioux."

For it was easy to see that when the Sioux war canoes came down the lake, they would pass between the island and the mainland. Indeed, the small beach on which they now found themselves had often served as a campsite for travelers along this much used route. The ashes of old fires blackened the sand in several places, and the poles of an abandoned lean-to still stood.

If they remained where they were, in plain sight of passing canoes, the Sioux would surely see them.

Kawa, who no doubt was thinking the same thing, called Wanito to him. "You must search the island for a place to camp," he said, "where we will be safe from the eyes of our enemy."

3

Wanito eagerly set out to do as his father had bid. He took his bow and a quiver of short Ojibway arrows, and began to climb the rocks that surrounded the beach. It was a hard climb, but the top of the island turned out to be quite flat and thickly covered with trees. Sometimes the forest floor was carpeted with thick moss that covered even the large boulders. Sometimes it was a tangle of fallen trees.

Now and then Wanito could see the water of Caribou Lake glinting in the sun far below. Finally he came to the end of the island, where the ground was quite smooth under a beautiful stand of pine trees. This, Wanito thought, would be a fine place to make their camp.

Then he remembered Kawa's twisted knee. His father would never be able to come this far over the rough ground. Besides, it would be dangerous to build a fire at such a high place, where it would be seen at a great distance after dark. Even in daytime, its smoke would be visible far down the lake.

Wanito decided it was not a good place to camp, after all. He set out on his return, going by a different way, and always looking for a flat, well-concealed spot where a shelter might be built and a fire made without fear of the Sioux's sharp eyes.

His path took him through a dense growth of fir trees near the edge of the island. "There should be spruce hens here," he said to himself, and fitted an arrow to his bow. Soon he had knocked half a dozen fat birds off the lower branches of the trees. Spruce hens were very stupid. They sat and looked at you with their round eyes wide open, although they seemed to be asleep.

Just before Wanito arrived back at the beach, he discovered the campsite he had been looking for. It was in a dense thicket of alders, where a small clearing had at one time been cut. An old *cingobigan,* an overnight shelter, occupied the site. It was so near the beach that when Wanito shouted, Nitana heard and answered him. Yet it was well concealed and, unless the Sioux landed on the beach itself, they would be quite safe there.

4

Wanito found his mother and sister busily spreading everything on the rocks to dry in the sun — blankets, clothing, even the water-soaked food. There was not much of that, except a small bag of rice and a few strips of smoked deer meat. So Odena welcomed Wanito's plump spruce hens with exclamations of delight. She kindled a small fire with some dry wood she had found, and soon the plucked birds were roasting over the coals and giving off delicious smells.

Everybody felt much better with a stomach full of warm food. They began to talk more hopefully about their situation. They even laughed when Waboos chased a bold moose-bird away from their drying rice. Then they began to plan what they might do next.

"The first thing," Kawa said, "is to cover the *cingobigan* you have found, Wanito, with some fresh balsam boughs. Then, at least, we shall have shelter."

"Nitana and I will do that," Odena said. "It is a woman's work."

"Then," Kawa continued, "we must think about food — for who knows how long we might be here?"

"The woods are full of spruce hens," Wanito said. "I can shoot as many as we need."

"And I can pick berries," Nitana piped up. "I saw lots of them on the rocks."

Kawa did not have to remind anyone that they must all do their part. Every Indian family knew that unless they worked together, all might starve, or freeze, or be killed by some wild beast or enemy. For life in the wilderness was hard and often cruel.

So they did not waste any time in covering the *cingobigan*. Wanito quickly cut a supply of balsam boughs and soon the shelter was roofed by a thick thatch, with enough boughs left over to make a deep, springy bed.

After that, they built a small fireplace of rocks. Wanito placed a pole over it between two forked sticks, from which to hang the kettle. Then they tidied up the beach, stowing away the blankets and clothing, which were now quite dry. Finally, they hid the wreckage of their canoe in the bushes, so that it would not be seen by anyone passing the island.

Kawa examined the remains of the canoe carefully. It was not quite a total loss. Although everything else was shattered, only a few of the ribs, the toughest part of the canoe, were broken.

"That is good," Kawa said. "We must save them."

Odena and Wanito wondered what he meant, but they were too exhausted to ask.

They all slept soundly that night on their bed of sweet-smelling balsam boughs, and awoke to a bright day, greatly refreshed.

5

As they made plans for the new day, their spirits rose and they became almost gay. They had not yet escaped from the Sioux, of course, and there was no way in which they could leave the island on which they had been wrecked. Still, they had been in worse trouble than this.

None of them, not even Nitana, had forgotten the terrible time of starvation three winters before. With Kawa sick and Wanito too young to hunt, they had lived for days on nothing but soup made from old fish bones that burned their lips and mouths, and gave them no strength. Then, after they had eaten the roasted leather of their moccasins and were too weak to gather firewood, a relative named Curly Bear came to their freezing lodge with half the carcass of a deer he had killed. And so they had been saved.

"It is enough," Odena said, remembering that dreadful time, "that we are alive and together — and that we have Wanito to hunt meat for us."

But Kawa, who from time to time had swept the surface of the lake with his keen eyes, suddenly thrust out his neck and peered intently at the horizon. Then they all saw it — a flash of something on the water, and again . . . and again . . .

It was the flash of wet canoe paddles in the sun. In a little while, the canoes themselves would come into sight.

Whose canoes?

There was no need for them to ask each other. They were all thinking the same thing. They were all thinking: *the Sioux!*

"Let us get out of sight," Kawa said quietly. "But first we must put out the fire."

They scraped sand furiously over the smoking embers. Then they hurried to the clearing in the alder thicket, Wanito and Odena half carrying Kawa between them. When they were safely concealed by the thick bushes, Kawa said: "They may be friends, or they may be Sioux. If they are Sioux, perhaps they will pass without noticing anything."

"I am sure they will," Odena said. "The beach is empty."

"But they may come here to make camp," Kawa continued. "In that case, you must all go to the other end of the island and look for a place to hide. The Sioux will find me, and I will tell them that the rest of my family was lost in the storm."

"No, Kawa!" Odena cried. "We will take you with us."

"There will be no time," Kawa said impatiently. "I cannot walk, and so I cannot expect to save myself. I will sing my death song and be happy if the rest of you escape."

Odena began to weep, and Nitana ran to her and buried her face in her mother's breast. Wanito stood silently before his father, at a loss for anything to say. Kawa spoke wisely, he knew; his plan was the only one that might save any of them. Yet, how could he leave his father alone?

"Maybe it is not the Sioux," he said at last. "Let me look again."

Without waiting for Kawa to answer, he climbed

a point of rocks jutting out into the water, and crouched down between two boulders. The paddle flashes were brighter now, and soon Wanito could see that they came from only one canoe. Then the form of the canoe itself became plain: it was Ojibway.

The discovery gave him a little surge of joy — until he remembered that the Sioux were no doubt traveling in canoes they had taken from his people.

But whether it was filled with Ojibway or Sioux, this canoe was keeping a straight course down the lake. It was not going to land at the island. Wanito returned to the hideout and told Kawa what he had seen.

"Look closely as they pass," Kawa said. "If they are friends, hail them."

By the time Wanito had returned to his lookout, the mysterious canoe was almost directly opposite the beach. Wanito could see the people in it quite clearly. They were not Sioux. They were not Indians. They were two bearded white men. And a dog sitting on the packs in the middle of the canoe.

Wanito waved his arms and shouted as loudly as he could. Odena and Nitana joined their shrill voices with his. But the traders' canoe kept close to the far shore, and not even the dog paid any heed to all their waving and shouting.

Finally, one of the traders looked across the open water. He said something to his companion, then raised a dripping paddle in a kind of greeting. The dog barked a couple of times. Then the canoe glided silently behind a small island and was gone.

For a while they gazed across the empty lake in dismay, as if they half expected the traders' canoe to appear again. But it was gone, they knew. It was gone for good.

"Now what shall we do?" Odena asked.

Kawa looked up quickly. Could it be that even Odena had lost heart?

"Do not be cast down," he said. "Before long we shall leave this island. Soon we shall be at the trader's fort and safe from the Sioux."

Odena and Wanito were too puzzled to answer him. They wondered if Kawa was speaking these brave words just to give them hope and courage. Finally Odena asked, "But how can we leave, Kawa? We cannot walk, and we have no canoe."

"We will build one," Kawa said.

To build a canoe, he reminded them, they needed only a few things that the forest would provide: some birch bark, the wood of a few cedar trees, the roots of a tamarack, and a little pitch.

"I have my crooked knife," he said. "With it I will

shape the wood. Odena has her canoe awl; she will sew the bark. And you, Wanito, have the ax; you can cut the cedars down and strip the birch tree of its bark."

"What can I do?" Nitana asked. "Is there nothing at all for me to do?"

"Yes, my daughter," Kawa said. "You can collect the pitch for gumming our new canoe."

"Do you hear that, Ona?" Nitana asked, very pleased. "We have important work to do."

So they were all cheerful again, and full of hope, and eager to carry out the tasks Kawa had given them. Even Waboos seemed to sense that some kind of great undertaking was afoot. He jumped up and yelped, as if to say, "Well, let's get on with it!"

But when they were all ready to set out, Kawa, who could only wait for them to return, looked at them sadly and said, "There is one thing more. If you hear me shout, do not come back. Wherever you are, look at once for a place to hide yourselves."

the visitor

1

Wanito recalled a grove of white cedars he had passed while searching for a campsite. He returned to it now, selected half a dozen straight young trees, and cut them down with his ax. He also lopped an armful of branches from some older trees.

After Wanito had trimmed the young cedars of their branches, Kawa set to work with his crooked knife. Kawa was the best canoe maker in his band — which made him a very important man among his people. The Ojibway could travel almost nowhere except by water, and a good strong canoe was often a matter of life or death.

The only tool Kawa required to build a canoe was his crooked knife. It had a sharp, curved blade with a rawhide handle, and looked like this:

Selecting one of the cedar branches Wanito had brought him, Kawa began to fashion a canoe rib. He grasped his knife in his right hand, palm upward, and drew it toward him. Long curling shavings of bark and wood rolled from under the keen blade. Soon he had completed the rib — a long strip of white wood, flat on one side and rounded on the other. It was about a finger thick and two fingers wide.

It was necessary to make only a few more. Luckily, most of the ribs in the old canoe proved sound enough for use in the new one. This saved not only much labor, but also precious time, in building the new canoe. Kawa quickly had all the ribs he needed, ready to be steamed and bent into the proper U-shape.

While Kawa was thus busy with his crooked knife, Odena was searching for tamarack trees from whose roots she could make *watap,* the tough fiber cord she would need for sewing the sheets of birch bark together. When she had found some, she called to Wanito to come and help her rip the tough roots from under the thin soil.

Before long, Odena had a large bundle of roots. She carried them to the beach and washed them in the clear water of the lake. Then, selecting a root about as long as her arm and as thick as a cattail reed, she grasped it between the fingers of both hands and carefully pulled it apart, so that it split into halves. Next she stripped the bark off each half with her teeth. In just a few moments, she had two pieces of smooth, white "cord" with which to sew birch bark or lash pieces of wood together.

In the meantime, Nitana was looking for trees from which she could collect pitch for gumming the seams of the canoe. Finally at the edge of the island, she discovered a grove of black spruce trees from which the golden pitch fairly oozed. She scraped the sticky "bubbles" onto a chip of cedar wood.

"That is very good," Odena said. "The best pitch comes from trees near the water."

They were all quite happy that their work was going so well, and they were even happier when Wanito caught three large fish off the rocks. They broiled the fish on the coals and had a good meal just as the sun was setting across the water.

Then they sat around their fire for a time and talked over their situation.

"Tomorrow," Kawa said, "you will find us some good birch bark, Wanito. Then we can begin to build our canoe, as Winabojo has taught us."

He said this lightly — as if birch bark fit for a canoe was easy to come by, as if you could find good canoe birches growing almost anywhere. But both Odena and Wanito knew that Kawa was not as sure of himself as he tried to sound. In the minds of both of them — and, no doubt, in Kawa's too — was the question: *What if no birches grow on this small island? What if we cannot find any birch bark for our canoe?*

2

Next day their fears became very real. Wanito searched the whole island without finding a single birch tree with bark suitable for canoe-making.

Once his hopes rose when he saw several tall, white trunks in the midst of a growth of young poplars. But they turned out to be the trunks of birches long ago destroyed by fire. Their wood was punky inside the silvery bark, and Wanito could push them over with one hand. Other dead birches lay on the ground, half covered with moss and lichens. But there was not a live one to be found.

Weary and hungry, Wanito gave up the search and started for camp. On his way, he passed through the grove of firs where he had killed the spruce hens. But, strangely enough, there was not a bird to be seen.

At the beach he found his family as busy as a colony of beavers. Kawa was now fashioning long, thin strips of cedar wood with which to line the canoe. Odena had a fine supply of *watap* soaking in the lake. And Nitana proudly displayed a *makuk* almost filled with the pitch she had gathered.

Only Wanito had nothing to show.

Nobody asked him whether he had found any bark; they all knew he hadn't. When he sat down on a flat rock beside the fire and stared into the flames, Nitana came and seated herself beside him.

"May I comb your hair, Wanito?" she asked.

When Wanito did not answer, she produced a

trader's comb and groomed her brother's hair, and in this way tried to raise his spirits.

After he had rested a bit, Wanito got out the nettle-fiber line and fished off the rocks. But it was a day on which nothing seemed to go right. He succeeded in catching only one small fish. Odena boiled it with some wild rice and a small piece of smoked meat for their evening meal. There was hardly enough to dull their hunger.

This created another worry. It was not so great a worry as that of the Sioux, but Wanito could not help but think: *We are almost out of rations. What shall we do if the game and fish fail?*

He was still thinking about this when he climbed the rocks for a last look down the lake before turning in — and saw through the gathering darkness the distant glimmer of a campfire.

3

"If there is only one fire," Kawa said, "that is good. It is not a war party. It may be some of our own people."

"Or it is another party of traders," Odena said hopefully. "And they will have room for us in their canoe. The white traders have very large canoes."

They were all greatly excited. Perhaps help was on the way at last. Perhaps in the morning they would escape from their island.

"At least they can take word to our relations at Pine Island to come for us," Kawa said.

They spoke of the various possibilities, and the more they discussed them, the more their hopes rose.

"Let us quit talking," Odena said at last, "and get everything ready to leave in the morning."

Kawa agreed with this: "The white men start early when they travel. They will be on their way before the sun is up. We will have to be ready."

"Yes," Odena said. "We must be sure we are not asleep when they pass."

"Don't worry," Wanito told his mother. "I will stay here on the beach, and keep watch for them."

He began at once to build up the fire and prepared to spend the night beside it. The air grew suddenly cold, and he knew that if he fell asleep the night chill would arouse him when the fire died down. Indeed, he awoke several times and went in search of more firewood. The last time was just before daybreak.

Wanito climbed up to his lookout and tried to see through the gloom and mist that covered the water. He could see no sign of a fire at the end of the lake. He wondered if the people who had been camping there were already on their way — if they might have passed while he was asleep.

He was struck with a feeling of guilt — of having broken his promise to keep a good watch. Somewhere, far out on the lake, a loon mocked him with its crazy laughter.

Then, looming large in the first light of day, the dim form of a canoe emerged. It seemed to be moving not on the surface of the water, but in midair over the mist-shrouded lake.

Wanito hurried down from his lookout and dashed to the *cingobigan*. He woke up everyone with excited shouts. The canoe was much nearer now, and it looked much smaller. The first rays of the sun glinted on the paddle of a single paddler. Suddenly he swerved from his course and headed directly for the island.

4

They all watched the man land his canoe. Neither Kawa nor Odena spoke a word, and Wanito wondered why they were so quiet.

Finally, as the man climbed out of his canoe — which was a very small one — and pulled it onto the beach, Kawa said: "It is Annooch."

Wanito had heard of Annooch, whose Ojibway name meant Squint Eye. He was well known among the Indians and also to the traders. The traders called him by the French name of Crapaud, that is, Toad. And nobody spoke well of him.

Wanito observed this man of whom he had heard so much evil. He was a small man, with half closed eyes and a face that, sure enough, reminded one of a toad. He was darker than a white man, yet he was not an Indian. He was, in fact, half of each.

Annooch's father was a French *voyageur*, his

mother an Ojibway woman. So he was half Ojibway by birth. But he had married a Sioux wife, and that made him a Sioux by marriage.

Nobody really knew how Annooch managed to make out in his strange, mixed-up Sioux-Ojibway-white world. He did not trap much, and he was a notoriously bad hunter. In addition, he was lazy and often the worse for firewater. Yet, he passed freely between enemy tribes and among rival white traders, and somehow found ways to survive — mostly, it was well known, by stealing, cheating, and lying. And more than once, it was rumored, he had not stopped at murder.

As Annooch approached, Wanito noticed that he carried his gun in the crook of his arm. A smile only made his ugly features more ugly.

"*Bojo, nitchee,*" he said in the Ojibway greeting. "Good day, friend."

"*Bojo,*" Kawa answered briefly.

Annooch looked around with a deliberate, curious air.

"How did you come here?" he asked. "I see no canoe."

Kawa did not answer him. Instead, he asked, "What do you want, Annooch?"

"I want nothing," Annooch said. "Only to help you."

"We need no help."

Annooch shrugged and smiled. His sharp squint eyes wandered to the bushes where the broken canoe was hidden.

"I can see that you are in trouble," he said. "I am sorry that my canoe is too small to take you off this island. He paused and smiled again. "Before the Sioux come."

"We do not fear the Sioux," Odena said defiantly. "They will never find us here."

"If they have eyes, they will," Annooch said. "Just as I have."

Then Annooch, it seemed, sought to frighten them by telling about the terrible havoc the Sioux had wreaked in Ojibway villages. "They leave nothing standing, growing, or breathing," he said. "They destroy even the dogs."

"Enough, Annooch," Kawa said. "Have you nothing better to do than frighten women and children?"

Nitana was crying and hiding behind her mother. "Yes!" Odena cried. "Go away, and let us be."

But then Annooch gave them some surprising news. The Sioux war band had met disaster on the Manitou Portage, he said. Two of their canoes had gone over the falls, and three warriors had drowned in the rapids below. Now they were waiting for another band to join them with fresh canoes.

If this was so, it was indeed good news! Several days, at least, would pass before the Sioux would take the war road again — days in which they could finish their canoe.

But was Annooch speaking the truth? Or was he telling them this only to raise false hopes and then dash them? Was it his cruel way of tormenting them — as a cat does a mouse? For he added, "But they will be along soon enough. They will not fail to call on you."

Annooch laughed loudly at his joke, which made Waboos bark at him furiously. Kawa looked up with a stony face.

"How do you know this?" he asked.

"I have just come from the Manitou Portage. The

Sioux are not my enemy, as they are yours, Kawa."

He laughed again and shifted his gun from the crook of his right arm to the left, with his finger resting near the trigger.

"I have also heard that you made a *cache* on the Otter of some fine beaver pelts. Is it true, Kawa?"

"That is no concern of yours, Annooch."

"True, *nitchee*," Annooch said, still smiling. "I only wish to help you. If you will tell me where you have hidden the furs, I will be glad to take them to a safe place — before the Sioux find them."

He paused, then added darkly, "Of course, if someone should tell the Sioux where you and your family are, they have ways to make you tell soon enough."

Wanito, who had been standing a little behind Annooch, saw what he was up to. He wanted to take the furs for himself. He would tell the Sioux where Kawa and his family were hiding, and then there would be nobody left to accuse him of his theft.

Wanito began to edge slowly toward the *cingobigan*, where he had left his bow and arrows. They would not be much good against Annooch's gun, he knew. But they were the only weapons they possessed.

And an Indian made the best of what he had.

5

Suddenly Annooch dropped his wheedling tone and his smile turned into an unpleasant scowl. His squint eyes rested for a while on the canoe ribs that Kawa had been fashioning.

"I see you are going to make a new canoe," he said. "Well, you might as well save yourself the trouble. You will never need a canoe again, Kawa."

He walked over to where Kawa lay beside his work. He kicked the canoe ribs in all directions. He picked up Odena's store of *watap* and hurled it into the bushes. Then he kicked Nitana's *makuk* of spruce gum and sent it spinning. Nitana cried out in horror and ran after it. Annooch laughed.

"Come, Kawa," he said. "Where are the furs?"

When Kawa still did not answer, he raised his gun halfway to his shoulder and took several steps toward Odena. He pointed the gun at her.

"I have no more time to waste," he said. "Tell me, or I will pull the trigger when I have counted the fingers on my right hand."

He began to count slowly — in the Ojibway tongue, so that Kawa would be sure to understand: *"Payshik . . . neesh . . . neesway . . . neon . . ."*

Just as he was about to count *narnan,* he was startled by the snapping of a twig behind him. He whirled about, his gun pointing skyward, to face Wanito. At the same instant, Wanito let fly from scarcely three paces away an arrow from his powerful Ojibway bow.

It was only a blunt arrow, such as the Ojibway hunted small game with. But so great was the force with which it sank into Annooch's midriff that the gun dropped from his hand as he doubled over, gasping for breath. Odena snatched it up. She backed away, beyond Annooch's reach, and held the muzzle steadily at his head.

Annooch straightened up, his mouth open, his chest heaving. When he had finally got back his wind, he pleaded: "Do not shoot me. I will not tell

the Sioux you are here. I swear it. Give me back my
gun and let me go."

Odena handed the gun, instead, to Wanito. Never
taking his eyes off Annooch, Wanito asked Kawa:
"What shall we do with this *sheecark?*"

Kawa was silent for a long time. Then he said
slowly, "I think we should put him on the Road of
Souls."

"No! No!" Odena cried. "We cannot kill even such a dog as Annooch, for his mother was of my own totem. He is of the eagle clan, as I am. So we cannot send him to another country."

Kawa was forced by tribal law to agree with Odena.

"Then we will spare his worthless life," he said. "But only if he will go to the trader's fort and send our relations to take us off this island."

"I swear I will do it," Annooch cried eagerly. "Give me my gun and I will go."

Now it was Kawa's turn to laugh.

"Are we fools, Annooch?" he asked. "You will take no gun and no ammunition with you. Nor anything to eat. Now what is your answer? Do you carry our message to the trader's fort?"

"I will carry the message," Annooch said glumly.

Without further words, he walked stiffly to his canoe. Wanito followed. Annooch tossed out his small store of dried meat and parched corn, then a horn of powder and a pouch of bullets.

"Do not betray us, Annooch," Wanito said sternly. "Unless you wish to change your climate."

Annooch gave Wanito a very ugly look, but without a word got into his canoe and paddled up the lake, toward the trader's fort.

"I think it best that we sent him away," Odena said, a little doubtfully.

"I am not so sure," Kawa answered. "I do not feel easy about him. He brings nothing but evil."

Wanito caressed the long gun he had taken from Annooch. "Now we have two guns," he said. "Now we can defend ourselves."

But then he remembered his father's words: "What could you and I do against so many?"

6

When Annooch's canoe finally disappeared in the mists of the lake, Kawa spoke reassuring words. Without food, he said, Annooch could not return to the Sioux and betray them. The distance was too great for a man to travel on an empty stomach. Besides, a strong wind was rising from the south, difficult to paddle against.

"He will have to go to the fort or starve," Kawa finished. "And perhaps to curry favor with the trader, he will tell our relations we are here."

Everybody felt a little better after this. Yet, who could tell, really, what such a wicked man might do?

They all got busy again, but with hearts far from light. Kawa continued to work with his crooked knife. Odena made more *watap* than would ever be needed. Nitana gathered enough pitch for two canoes.

But everyone knew that all this was useless without birch bark. Not even Winabojo could make a canoe without bark.

Wanito searched the island once more, to make sure he had not overlooked a birch tree somewhere. He returned to the *cingobigan* at dusk, empty-handed. Odena had caught a single fish off the rocks, and they made a poor meal of this and a little rice.

Nobody had much to say before they went to bed hungry and — although none admitted it — quite discouraged and a little afraid.

the spirit bird

1

WANITO DID NOT join his family in the *cingobigan*.
He climbed to his lookout and peered hard down the
lake, but he could see nothing in the darkness. Then
he rolled up in his blanket and lay down beside the
fire.

Almost at once, he entered that mixed-up world,
half real, half dream, in which people lose themselves just before they fall asleep. Pictures of the
Sioux crowded into his mind — shrieking demons in
war paint, tumbling out of their canoes and splash-
ing toward the island with knives and tomahawks

upraised. Then his thoughts drifted to a grove of tall, silvery trees — canoe birches, waiting to offer him their beautiful bark. As he wandered among them, trying to select the finest, a night bird screeched in the treetops and aroused him for a moment. Then he fell into a deep sleep.

It was near first light when he had his dream.

He dreamed he was in a dark spruce forest, so dense that he could hardly force his way through it. He was searching for something he could not find. He was very weary and hungry. And he was lost.

Suddenly he broke out of the deep woods onto a path filled with sunshine. Ahead of him, something hovered in the air. It was a small, white bird. It continued to fly just beyond his reach, its snowy wings flashing in the pure sunlight.

"Follow me," the little bird seemed to say, although in words that Wanito could not actually hear.

So he followed it out of the woods to the edge of a sparkling sheet of water, and across the water to another shore. It seemed to him that he floated through the air over the water, with the white bird always ahead of him.

When they reached land again, the bird suddenly vanished, and Wanito found himself standing in just such a fine grove of tall birch trees as he had imagined before he fell asleep. Yellow leaves were drifting down through beams of sunlight, and they rustled around his feet as he walked through them. He struck one of the birches with his hand — to see if it, like the trees he had found on the island, might not be rotten. But it was hard and sound, and the blow stung his hand. It left a white powder on his palm, a sure sign the bark was thick and good — the kind the Ojibway called *djimanicig*.

2

Wanito woke up as suddenly as if someone had shaken him. He jumped out of his blanket and looked around, uncertain of where he actually was. He stared at his hand, to see if it was white with the powder of *djimanicig*. Little by little the details of his dream came back to him, and he was filled with a mystical excitement.

For to have such a dream was about the most eventful thing that could happen to an Indian boy. All Indians took their dreams very seriously. When an Indian child went to bed, his parents would say, "Try to dream, and remember what you dream." This was to accustom him to dreaming, and to make him understand how powerful dreams were.

When an Indian boy was about to become a man, he would go into the woods alone and fast, sometimes for days, to bring dreams that would guide him in life. Often he dreamed what his name was to be. If he dreamed of an animal — a bear or wolf, perhaps — he would call on that animal in danger or in battle, and it would protect him. Sometimes people even believed that they entered another spirit world in their dreams.

So Wanito knew that his dream had a very important meaning. It did not take him long to decide what it was: *If he crossed water, he would find birch bark for a canoe.*

Then he remembered that sometimes Winabojo himself appeared to people in dreams — in the form of a little white spirit bird. And he was sure that if he crossed over to the mainland, Winabojo would lead him to the canoe birches he had seen in his dream.

He lost no time in doing what the spirit bird had instructed him to do. He belted his skinning knife to his waist. Then he hung his ax around his neck with a loop of *watap*. It was almost light now, and he could see that the lake was smooth and quiet. He slipped into the water and struck out for the mainland shore.

Like all Ojibway, who lived their lives on or near water, Wanito was a strong swimmer. The island quickly fell behind him, and he had not even begun to tire when he pulled himself out of the lake onto the rocky shore.

He quickly found an opening in the black spruce forest that came down to the water line, and began to climb toward higher ground. He was uncertain which way to go. He wished that the little white spirit bird would appear and guide him. But nothing except a chickadee flew up ahead of him, and vanished in an alder thicket. So he kept on climbing, pausing only long enough to gather a few raspberries on a fire-swept hillside. He was very hungry.

The sun was well above the treetops when the ground began to slope down again. He had not yet seen even a sapling birch. If he had not been an Ojibway, perhaps he might have begun to lose faith in his dream. But now something about the nature of the ground raised his hopes. The soil under his feet was no longer sandy and covered with pine needles. Red squirrels no longer chattered at him as he passed. The ground was black and damp, and covered with a layer of fallen leaves — the kind of soil in which birches grew. And he could smell water not far away.

Then he came to a high ledge of rock, and below it lay a beautiful grove of tall, white trees. A golden rain of leaves fell lazily from their lofty tops. The water of Caribou Lake shimmered between their snowy trunks.

3

There were so many lovely canoe birches in the grove that Wanito could not make up his mind which one to cut down. Finally, he selected a large tree with particularly smooth and heavy bark, and felled it with his ax.

The next step was to remove the bark from the trunk. This caused Wanito a little trouble, because in the fall of the year, the bark of a birch tightens around the trunk. The proper time to gather bark is in the spring, when it comes off the tree easily. But Wanito could hardly wait *that* long. So he worked away with his ax and knife, and after a while had as much bark as Kawa would need for a canoe. This he rolled up in wide strips, then tied the rolls together with some of the *watap* he carried in his belt.

The sun was halfway down the sky by the time Wanito had finished, but he was in no hurry. He would have to wait for cover of darkness before returning to the island. He did not want to risk being caught by the Sioux while crossing the lake in broad daylight. Besides, he had to think of a way to get the bark across.

He could swim with it tied to his back, a piece at a time. But that would be a long, slow way to do it, and he doubted that he could finish in one night. He looked for raspberries while he thought it over. Finally, he decided to make a little raft on which to ferry the bark to the island.

Because their wood was so light and buoyant, he cut down half a dozen young cedars, trimmed them, and bound them together with their own roots. Very soon he had a small raft, to which he lashed his rolls of bark. Then, having made sure of the direction he must swim in the darkness, he sat down and waited for night to fall.

As soon as it was too dark for him to see the island, he fastened the raft to the back of his belt with a long strip of *watap,* and started to tow it across. A light breeze from the mainland helped him a little, but it was still a slow, hard swim with the drag of the raft behind him. He thought of the muskrats he had often seen crossing a small lake in the moonlight with large green branches in their mouths. He was like one of those muskrats, he thought.

When at last he saw the glimmer of a campfire in the darkness, he knew that he was on the right course and would soon be with his family. They were keeping the fire up, he knew, to guide him home —

although they did not know where he had gone or what had happened to him. He felt sorry for the worry he must have caused them.

Then he thought with a sudden pride: *They need never be uneasy about me again, for haven't I proved myself a man, well able to take care of myself? . . . And of them, too, if need be.*

the canoe

1

ODENA COULD not stop exclaiming over the fine bark that Wanito had brought them.

"It is so beautiful," she repeated. "It is almost perfect. Where did you find it, Wanito?"

Wanito merely shrugged. He said nothing about the spirit bird. A man did not talk about his dreams.

Kawa said gruffly, "It is enough that he found it, Odena. Do not trouble him with questions."

But Odena knew that Kawa spoke in this way to hide the pride he felt for his son.

"Besides," Kawa added, "a pile of bark, no matter how fine, is not a canoe. We have a lot of work to do. Let us sleep a little now and get at it early in the morning."

The sun, indeed, was not yet up when they gathered at the spot Kawa had chosen for building the canoe. It was an open space near the water, free of brush and quite level. After Wanito had made it still smoother, Kawa told him to cut down small trees and make some stakes, sharpened at one end. When he had enough, Kawa said: "Good! Now we will build a canoe, as Winabojo has taught us to."

For the Ojibway believed that Winabojo, the Master of Life, had long ago taught them how to make many useful things — tipis, bows and arrows, snowshoes, nets, and most important of all, canoes.

The rules of canoe-making, learned from Winabojo, were very strict, and Kawa knew them all. He carried each of the necessary measurements in his head. He knew exactly how to fashion every part. And nobody in all the Ojibway nation made sturdier or more beautiful canoes than Kawa.

First, with a sharp stick, he traced the outline of a canoe on the ground that Wanito had smoothed

and leveled. It was three arm spreads long and
about an arm's length wide in the middle. Kawa
measured the distances precisely with "hand
spreads," the span from his thumb to the end of his
middle finger. When he had finished, the pattern of
the canoe looked like this:

Kawa made the front half of his pattern a bit wider
than the back half, so that the canoe would be shaped
a little like a fish. This would make it faster and
steadier in the water. It was a secret that only the
very best of canoe makers knew.

Next, Kawa directed Wanito to drive stakes along
the lines he had drawn on the ground. Like this:

While Wanito was doing this, Kawa continued to fashion long, flat strips of cedar wood from the splints that Wanito had made for him with his ax. He shaved and smoothed them with his crooked knife until they were almost as thin as strips of heavy birch bark. They would be used to line the canoe.

In the meantime, Odena and Nitana were busy preparing the bark. They scraped away the crumbly red layer of inner bark that lay next to the trunk, leaving the pale yellow surface clean and velvety smooth. Then they cut it into wide sheets, free from bad spots and holes through which the branches had grown.

When everything was ready, Odena called to Kawa that her work was finished. And now began the real building of the canoe.

2

First, Kawa selected two long, sturdy strips of cedar, and Odena fastened them with *watap* to the stakes Wanito had driven into the ground, curving each end upward. These strips would form the rim of the canoe. The Ojibway called them *bimikwan*. The "frame" of the canoe now looked like this:

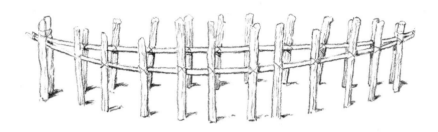

By the time all this was finished, darkness was closing in. Night fell suddenly at this time of year. All at once it was too dark, even by the light of the fire, for Odena to begin fitting and sewing the bark covering of the canoe.

They ate a scanty meal, since everyone had been too busy during the day to fish for food. Then Wanito climbed to his lookout. But he could see nothing at the dark end of the lake. So, although their stomachs were far from happy, they went to bed content enough. There was still no sign of the Sioux, and they had bark for their canoe.

3

There was a white frost on their blankets when they woke up next morning, and a chill wind was raising little whitecaps on the lake.

"Let us hope it will blow a gale," Kawa said. "The Sioux will not care to paddle against a head wind."

No Indians, indeed, not even the Ojibway, would venture into a strong wind blowing directly against them. Sometimes canoes would remain ashore, windbound for days, rather than face the toil and danger of battling a head wind. And the Sioux were notoriously poor canoemen.

"The Kitchi-Manitou is surely looking after us," Odena said cheerfully.

"Let us not count too much on the Manitou," Kawa said. "We cannot expect help from him unless we help ourselves."

This, of course, was Kawa's way of saying, "Let us stop talking and get on with our work." Everybody took the hint and even Nitana, who was still half asleep, got busy at once.

Now it was time for Odena to do the work that

women always performed. She chose two of the largest and best sheets of bark and dropped them crosswise, inside out, between the stakes at the middle of the canoe. Like this:

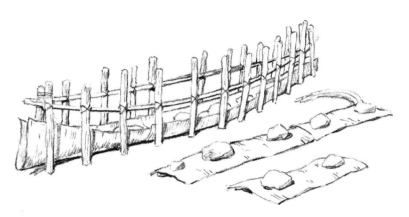

Then she laid more strips between the stakes, from end to end. Wanito now placed large, smooth stones on the bark to hold it tightly against the ground, forming the bottom of the canoe, while the rest of the bark turned up against the stakes to form the sides. Odena then trimmed the edges of the bark and rounded the ends to form the bow and stern of the canoe.

The next step was to sew the strips of bark together. Odena was so expert that her seams hardly needed gumming. She could sew a whole canoe, if need be, in a single day.

"Watch closely, now," she said to Nitana, "so you will know how to help your husband make a good canoe."

From the time they were very young, all Indian girls were taught by their mothers to do the work of a woman: to cook, make garments of leather and cloth, build a tipi and keep it clean, tan hides, and sew a canoe. So Nitana paid close attention to what her mother was doing.

The only tool Odena used was her canoe awl, called a *migos*. It was made of bone, slightly curved, with a handle of rawhide. It had been given to Odena by her own mother. Odena had used it so long that it seemed almost a part of her arm. This is how it looked:

With her *migos* Odena punched holes along the edges of the sheets of bark. Through the holes she then drew strands of *watap,* which had been soaking in the lake to make it soft and pliable. Odena plied her awl swiftly and skillfully, binding the sheets of bark neatly together. When she had finished, her work looked for all the world like a huge, canoe-shaped birch bark basket.

Odena had to work very fast, even with Nitana's help, to accomplish all this in a single day. By the time she finished, night had settled over the island. But the wind did not die down as it usually did after sunset. If anything, it blew harder. It scattered the smoke and ashes of their fire. Whitecaps on the lake gleamed through the darkness.

"The Wind Spirits are on our side," Kawa said. "They are keeping the Sioux far away from us."

But Kawa, alas, spoke too soon. What Wanito saw when, as usual, he climbed to his lookout at bedtime made his father's hopeful words sound like the mocking laughter of the loons.

For, at the very end of the lake, where the Otter River emptied into it, the fitful gleam of not one, but half a dozen fires flickered through the darkness. They could only be the campfires of the Sioux.

4

Now everything — their very lives — depended on finishing their canoe.

And on the wind.

It might blow for days without letup. Then, even with the Sioux camp in plain sight, they would have time to finish their canoe and escape.

Or it might die down suddenly — perhaps that very night.

"Then," Kawa asked grimly, "what good will a half-finished canoe do us?"

It was a hard question, with an answer that all knew but did not care to think about.

Silently they built up the fire, so they could work by its light. For there would be no sleep now.

Kawa showed Odena and Wanito what to do next — how to line the birch bark shell of the canoe with the long, thin strips of cedar he had already fashioned. They laid these strips close together on the bottom and against the sides of the bark, from one end to the other.

When it grew too dark to see well, even by the light of the fire, Odena made torches from scraps of pitched birch bark, tied to sticks and thrust into the ground. It was almost morning when they finished, for it was a slow, painful task fitting the pieces of cedar wood together.

"Good!" Kawa said, after inspecting their work. "Now eat a little meat for strength. You still have much to do."

So they chewed on strips of smoked deer meat, too weary to prepare a proper meal. When it grew light enough to see, Wanito dragged himself to his observation post for a look up the lake. But the spume whipped up by the gale made it impossible to see more than a few canoe lengths across the water.

The lake, indeed, was now swept by a storm even fiercer than the one that had dashed their canoe to pieces on the beach. And it was blowing straight in the teeth of the Sioux.

"I don't think this will let up very soon," Kawa said. "We can get a little sleep now."

5

But Wanito and Odena had scarcely closed their eyes, it seemed, before Kawa was shaking them and calling for them to wake up.

"The wind is dying down," he said anxiously. "We will have to get back to our work."

The alarm in his voice pulled them to their feet, and they hurried to the canoe. But the work that now had to be done — the placing of the ribs — was something that only Kawa knew how to perform properly. It was the most difficult step of all, and one of the most important. For if the ribs were not well set, the canoe might easily turn over in the water.

What Kawa could not do himself, with his twisted knee, he showed them how to do. One by one, they thrust the ribs crosswise into the shell of birch bark. The ribs curved snugly from rim to rim. They hugged the sides and bottom, pressing the thin strips of cedar sheathing tightly against the bark. As each was forced into place, Odena lashed its ends securely to the rim of the canoe with *watap*.

They worked in desperate haste, but they were inexpert and made mistakes that Kawa had to correct. So only half the ribs were in place by midday, when they stopped work long enough to eat a little rice and meat that Odena had set to boiling over the fire. Worse still, the wind continued to abate.

By sunset it had died down enough so that a very brave — or very foolish — man might have chanced launching a canoe against it. Almost surely, the Sioux would not take that risk. They knew little about the weather on large lakes, and even less about how to manage a canoe in a gale.

Yet, there was always the possibility of a sudden calm. Sometimes even the most violent storms "blew over" abruptly, leaving blue skies and quiet water behind them.

What if this should happen now?

This was the question that never left their minds as they struggled feverishly to finish the canoe on which their lives depended. They grew weak from hunger and want of sleep, and their fingers bled. But the building of the canoe went forward, far into the night again, by torch and firelight.

Finally, all the ribs were set. An outer rim was bound firmly in place. Crossbars, or thwarts, were lashed across the middle and near the ends to brace the framework. It was near morning again when Kawa, noting that the wind still blew strongly toward the Sioux camp, said: "Enough for now."

They dropped where they stood and were asleep.

escape

_____

1

WANITO AWOKE in broad daylight. He went immediately to his lookout, to see what the Sioux might be up to. This time he carried with him the gun they had taken from Annooch, with its horn of powder and pouch of bullets.

The mist had cleared from the lake, so that he could see the Sioux encampment quite clearly. Several fires were burning on the small beach at the mouth of the Otter. There appeared to be several stolen Ojibway canoes upturned on the shore.

And one on the lake!

The canoe on the lake was coming toward the island. It was making but slow progress, however. The wind was rising again, and the water was rough enough to make heavy labor of paddling. The canoe was heading directly into the wind. The waves were heaving it up and down, and Wanito could see with what force the bow hit the water after cresting each roller.

"Clumsy Sioux canoemen!" Wanito said to himself. "You will be lucky if you don't break in two."

He wondered what they were doing on the lake in such weather. Could they have seen their fire on the island? Were they trying to come closer, even in such a fierce head wind, to find out who was camped there?

Then he recognized the bow paddler. It was Annooch!

So that answered his question. Instead of going to the trader's fort, Annooch had turned back. Somehow he had managed to reach the Sioux encampment on the Manitou Portage. Now he was trying to lead the Sioux to the island.

Wanito examined the priming of his gun, making

sure that the powder pan was well filled. He had never fired a long gun with a full load before, but he was sure he could do it as well as his father. He rested the barrel on a rock and sighted on Annooch.

The canoe was still too far away to risk a shot. It would have to come much closer before he could hope to hit such a bobbing, pitching target.

He waited patiently, sighting from time to time on the paddlers. He would have to disable only one. A canoe with only one paddler would founder at once in such a sea. Perhaps it would be enough just to blow a hole in the canoe. And if he missed the first shot, there would be plenty of time to reload and fire again, and again.

Raising his eyes, he could see that a little group of Sioux in war gear were watching the canoe from their camp. What a chance to humiliate the enemy! Wanito fairly ached with a desire to get Annooch in his sights and pull the trigger.

But he could see that Annooch and his canoe mate were getting into worse and worse trouble. Their canoe was taking a great deal of water. It was in constant danger of swamping. Suddenly it made a desperate turnabout between rollers, just barely avoiding a fatal upset. Then the gale swept it back to shore.

Wanito could imagine the derisive shouts of the Sioux watchers.

When he returned to the *cingobigan,* he found all his family awake and eager to finish work on the canoe. He told his father quietly about Annooch.

"So now the Sioux know where we are," Kawa said. "Well, let us not fear anything. We are safe as long as this wind lasts."

But, despite Kawa's confident words, who could say for sure how long that would be?

2

"Now we can pull up the stakes," Kawa said.

This was the work of only a few minutes. When it was finished, the canoe, now all but completed, seemed to float on the ground where it had been built. So graceful were its lines, so lovely was the pattern that Winabojo had taught his people to follow!

Only the gumming of the seams remained, and this was woman's work — work for Odena and Nitana.

Odena heated the pitch Nitana had gathered and added a bit of powdered charcoal to give it body. Then she spread it on the seams of the birch bark with a little wooden paddle. It did not take her long to make the whole canoe watertight, for she had sewn it so well that gumming was hardly needed.

While Odena was at work, Wanito went on a

meat hunt. He took his bow and arrows and returned to the grove of fir trees where he had killed
the spruce hens. There he found a flock scratching
in the ground for their morning meal. They paid no
attention to him when he approached, and he easily
knocked over five of them with his blunt arrows.

So they had a fine meal of roasted birds, with all
that was left of their store of wild rice and blueberries.

"We will have our next meal in our village," Kawa
said.

Then, with full stomachs, they sat beside their
fire and waited for the wind to die down.

"Let us see if we can get a sign from the Wind
Spirits," Kawa said to Nitana. "Let us see if they
will tell you when the lake will be quiet."

For the Ojibway believed that children could
learn things from the Nature Spirits that grownups
were never told — that they had ways of coaxing the
Spirits to give them information.

"Yes," Odena said, "let us make a little medicine."

She drew a strand of *watap* from the hank she
always carried in her belt, and quickly made a little

boatlike dish from a scrap of leftover birch bark. Then Kawa placed in the dish a pinch of tobacco, and Wanito added a flea contributed by Waboos. Kawa handed the dish to Nitana.

"Take it down to the water," he said, "and set it afloat in a quiet place."

Nitana did as she was told. She carefully launched the little craft on a tiny sheet of smooth water between some rocks. The wind caught it, whirled it about, then carried it into open water. A wave quickly overturned it, spilling the tobacco and the flea into the lake.

Then everybody laughed and shouted, and Waboos yelped excitedly. For this was a sure sign that the wind was about to die down, and they could soon resume their journey.

3

It began to grow dark.

"The moon is rising," Odena said, pointing to a faint glow beyond the hilltops. "We shall have a good light to travel by."

They all watched silently as the big orange disk of the autumn moon swam into the sky. When it was high enough to throw a shimmering path across the lake, they could see that Nitana's spirit boat had indeed told them the truth. For suddenly the water was almost smooth.

"Come!" Kawa cried. "We must be on our way while the Sioux are asleep."

They hastily wrapped their gear in a blanket, and Wanito carried it down to the shore. They carefully set the canoe in the water, and were ready to leave.

"First we must thank the Kitchi-Manitou," Kawa said, "for saving us from the Sioux."

"And Winabojo," Odena added.

So Kawa raised his eyes to the sky and chanted a prayer to both the Manitou and Winabojo. When he had finished, everyone got into the canoe and, without a backward glance, they glided onto the moonlit expanse of Caribou Lake.

Only Waboos made the slightest sound. He barked dutifully a couple of times, then curled up and went to sleep beside Ona in Nitana's lap.

Since Kawa was not yet able to paddle, Wanito took the stern of the canoe, while Odena worked in the bow. Wanito guided the canoe at once toward the mainland, where the water was smoothest along the shore and the shadows deep. As they crossed the narrow strip of water, they could see the glow of the distant Sioux camp.

"They are asleep beside their fires," Kawa said. "Before they wake up, we will be at the trader's fort."

Wanito could not repress an urge to cast a few departing insults at the enemy.

"Tame cats! Old women!" he shouted. "Try and catch us now!"

Their canoe carried them swiftly along the shadowy border of the lake. With each quick, strong stroke of the paddles, it seemed to fly over the water. It gave Wanito a feeling of pride to know that he had helped to make such a fine canoe.

4

As the sun came up, they could see the stockade and watch tower of the trader's fort on a high bank above the portage. The great gate of the fort was already opened as if to welcome them to the protection of strong walls. And, as they drew nearer, people began to run down to the water's edge from the cluster of tipis in the shadow of the stockade. They were curious, no doubt, to know who might be approaching at such an early hour.

Then, when Kawa and his family were close enough to be recognized, the little crowd began to shout. Dogs barked and Waboos barked back. Their relations rushed into the water and drew their canoe ashore. Everyone was chattering and laughing, and embracing one another, and some of Odena's relations were crying. For the people in the village had been sure that Kawa and all his family had been killed — as Big Turtle had told them — by the Sioux.

The master of the fort, whose name was Angus Mackenzie, also came down to the landing and welcomed them, for Kawa and Odena were both highly respected by the traders.

"You were lucky to escape the Sioux," Mackenzie said. "Not all of your people were so fortunate."

He talked pleasantly with them and invited them to come into the fort for supplies and food. Then he bent over to examine the overturned canoe in which they had just arrived. He gave the creamy yellow bark of its bottom an approving thump with his open hand.

"I see you have a new canoe, Kawa," he said. "It is a fine one. Would you like to sell it?"

Kawa smiled and looked at Wanito the way people do when they share a secret.

"I cannot sell it, my friend," he answered very seriously. "It is a present — from Winabojo."